Sid froze. He made a sign for Russel to come forward and Russel silently crept up to where he could see what Sid saw.

Between the trees they could see an old man just sitting on the ground looking exhausted. He wore a dingy red and white suit, a big red hat, big black belt and black boots. The man had an unkempt white beard, but other than a general state of dirt and grime, he looked for all the world like pictures Russel had seen of Santa Claus when he was younger, before the zombies came and their lives had changed overnight.

RUSSEL AND SID ADVENTURE BOOKS

RUSSEL AND SID SAVE SANTA FROM ZOMBIES

Series Created and Written by

Patrick Kilhoffer

Cover Art

Trees through fog photo by Kevin Kilhoffer

© Kevin Kilhoffer Photography 2015

Zombie Silhouettes designed by Freepik

Santa Designed by Kjpargeter freepik.com

Pigweed/Amaranth USDA-NRCS PLANTS Database / USDA NRCS. Wetland flora: Field office illustrated guide to plant species. USDA Natural Resources Conservation Service.

Cattails by Pearson Scott Foresman

Acorns extracted from the book Vom Kaukasus

zum Persischen Meerbusen 1897 Author Unknown

Baby Zombie by Aleisha Engness

Published by Washmet Publishing, LP

© Washmet Publishing, LP 201

ISBN: 978-0-9971581-4-4

First printing October 2016

Printed in the U.S.A.

Chapter 1

Russel closed his journal and tucked it inside his inside jacket pocket. Outside, the sun had just gone down and the air was clear and cold. The full moon cast bright shadows on the thin fresh layer of snow.

Every time Russel found an

edible plant, he made a note of where it was so they could come back and harvest it later. He had written down descriptions in the fall of where the sunchoke, a kind of wild potato, was growing and now it was time to harvest it.

In the winter, all the nutrients were stored in the roots of the sunchoke plant until it was ready to sprout again in the spring. Or, in the case of these particular plants, keep two young men fed through the winter. And this particular sunchoke patch was huge. If they kept getting lucky hunting and trapping raccoons, squirrels, and rabbits, the sunchoke patch would last until spring.

Russel went over to the small wood stove that heated the tiny cabin and added more water and some dried herbs to the big pot that was simmering, before stirring the pot with an old spoon. There were some bits of meat, but mostly it was bones and water. It had been 3 days since they caught a raccoon and they were down to just boiling the carcass over and over to get broth to drink.

Lately they weren't catching as many raccoons, and Russel wondered if they hadn't finally caught them all. Hopefully they would get a rabbit tonight, or they would return from their hike to find they had caught another raccoon in a trap.

Sometimes they caught opossum, but the boys hadn't been that hungry yet. Their dad always said if the choice was between eating opossum and being hungry, he would eat opossum and smile.

"But Dad wasn't here," Russel thought pushing his memories away, "and opossums are *gross*."

It wasn't that Russel was particularly picky about what he ate. No one could afford to be these days if they wanted to survive. He ate coyotes when his dad shot them, even though they looked like dogs. He ate squirrels whenever Sid shot one, but opossum meat had a gamey taste to it that he never could get used to.

"Even if we don't catch anything, adding the sunchoke roots we are going to get tonight with the broth from the bones will make a good meal," he thought, his stomach gurgling at the thought of having a full belly for a change.

Russel picked up the shovel and food bag, hooked the hatchet on his belt and slung the emergency bag over his shoulder. The emergency bag had the stuff they couldn't afford to lose in case someone was at their camp when they returned. If they had to, they could walk away and start fresh somewhere else. The bag was noticeably lighter than it was a few months ago as their supplies got used up. Russel tried not to think about how little the bag still had in it.

He put some more wood in the stove and closed the damper so it would stay burning all night.

The boys didn't have a lot of warm clothes and Russel was very aware that every match they used might never be replaced.   After studying the stove for a moment he decided it was time to get to work.

The zombies weren't going to give them any trouble at night when it was this cold, and they hadn't seen another person for weeks. Before that, the few people they had seen had been a half mile away and headed away from them.

"Come on Sid." Russel said, forcing a smile at his younger brother. "It's time to get to work."

Sid stood up from where he had been working on making a fish trap and carefully set the half-finished project to one side. It would likely take him several more days to make a fish trap from the green branches he was using, but once it was done it would hopefully let them catch more fish.

They had one fish trap already, and that caught a fish once a week or so from the small river a few hundred yards from the cabin. There was a small stream that was closer to the cabin that they got their drinking water from but there were never any fish in it, just an occasional small frog that followed the stream up from the river.

"You can take point with the bunny gun if you want," Russel spoke again, "maybe we can have some meat in the stew tonight."

Sid didn't say anything in reply, but Russel knew his brother well enough that he hadn't been expecting him to. Sid rarely talked if he didn't have to. Russel checked the fire one more time to make sure it would stay burning until they got back.

Sid picked up the pellet rifle and the small box of pellets and double checked that the safety was on before loading a pellet and quietly cocking it. He put the box of pellets in his pocket and nodded that he was ready.

Sid was deadly accurate with the pellet rifle and they had plenty of pellets, but rabbits were scarce. They were more likely to get a raccoon or squirrel but sometimes they got lucky.

Russel's mouth watered at the thought of roasted rabbit, but he knew they weren't likely to see one at night. Still, it was safer to move at night when the zombies weren't as active and most people were asleep or at least settled down for the night.

Russel carefully shut the door on the cabin after Sid walked through the doorway. Letting the door slam shut could be heard a long way away, and the boys had learned the hard way that zombies had were attracted to any unusual noises.

The boys walked to the fence and Russel tightened the loop that held the makeshift gate shut after he and Sid walked through. Their cabin was surrounded by a fence made of scavenged wire, rope, branches and anything else they could find that would stop a zombie from just walking right up to their cabin.

The only good thing about zombies was they were really stupid. They would walk right up to the fence and just keep trying to push their way forward. As long as you had a good fence and were careful, you could hit them in the head with a machete or hatchet while they stood there.

Other humans were often a bigger threat than the zombies were. Russel wished briefly they had a way to hide their footprints but with the freshly fallen snow, there wasn't much he could do to hide them.

Most people realized that the more bartering they did and the fewer fights they got in, the longer they would live. But sometimes people got desperate and there were always raiders to worry about.

By now, the people that

couldn't figure out how to stay alive were pretty much gone, but raiders either didn't know how to trap and hunt or didn't want to. They counted on raiding abandoned houses to get food. If they found someone living there, sometimes they would break in and steal the food, or worse.

Russel pushed the thought of raiders away before his memories filled in what all "worse" entailed. Other people traveled and bartered scarce items for food and supplies but they were few and far between.

"But even most of them would raid when they thought they could get away with it." Russel reminded himself. The boys counted on the dense woods and difficult terrain that surrounded their cabin to keep them hidden from other people, raiders or not.

"You can't lose a fight you aren't in. Your best chance is to avoid a fight. The best way to avoid a fight is to avoid other people. If there is any doubt in your mind at all, stay hidden." his Dad had instructed the boys before he left weeks ago.

They were always careful to stay quiet and they tried not to walk too far from the cabin during the day.

Sid looked back to make sure Russel would be following, and then silently walked into the woods. As always, Russel walked slowly enough that Sid stayed 50 feet in front, close enough that Russel could see him and anyone close to him in the moonlight, but far enough away that someone else wouldn't be able to easily shoot both of them.

Russel scanned left and right as he walked, his nose stinging from the cold, as he looked for anything that might be a threat or food.

Russel couldn't help but notice Sid's gait was somewhat uneven at times, and he appeared that he was sometimes wincing as he walked. Sid didn't complain but Russel knew that after 3 years wearing the same shoes Sid's feet had to have outgrown his current pair.

As they walked, Russel tried to decide if it made sense to try to scavenge more clothes or other supplies from some of the deserted houses that remained within a day's walk. Most of the houses in the towns and cities had burned down after the fire departments stopped operating, and many of the remaining had zombies trapped inside or desperate people living in them.

Often, people would burn down a house accidentally by trying to build a fire to keep warm. Other times people started the house on fire intentionally to kill the zombies or even the people inside.

During the Crazy Year, the street gangs were burning down any house or building that they suspected a rival gang might be in. Soon most houses were abandoned because it was too obvious of a target to try to live in. After a couple of years, the few remaining empty homes tended to be stripped clean of anything usable.

But sometimes you got lucky. The houses in the country were harder to get to and were more likely to still have usable items inside and with the snow on the ground, the lack of footprints would make it easier to see if the houses were really unoccupied. Even something that could be made into something usable was better than nothing.

If they didn't find any shoes maybe they would find something Russel could make into a pair of moccasins, like the leather from a sofa.

"Maybe there would be some blankets." Russel shivered. It was the last week of December and it seemed like each night it got colder.

Russel worried a lot about his younger brother. He

watched Sid quietly move from tree to tree, pausing behind each tree to check for movement. Sid rarely spoke and almost never smiled lately. It was hard on both of them, but keeping them both alive kept Russel busy thinking about other things.

Sid just always seemed sad. Russel remembered playing with toys when he was Sid's age. But Sid didn't have any toys to play with, everything had to be left behind to make room for supplies and tools.

Sometimes Russel tried to make things more fun for his brother, but It was hard to play without making noise, and Russel was always either too busy or too tired after making sure they had enough food and firewood. There weren't any other kids their age around to play with or even just to talk to.

Russel knew that Sid missed their parents. He missed them too, but he missed reading the most. He kept a foraging journal so he could remember where edible plants were, and sometimes he would take it out and read it just to have something to read.

His dad promised to bring back some books if he could, but Russel knew that there weren't likely to be any books left. People were using the pages to start fires and burning them for heat to try to stay warm. By the end of the second winter there were very few books left anywhere.

Chapter 2

The two boys moved silently through the woods, drifting from tree to tree as they made their way to the spot Russel had put on his map. They walked past the little grove of maple trees that they had tapped for sweet sap in the spring.

Russel knew that it took a lot of firewood and time to boil the syrup to make the sweet sap into maple syrup and maple sugar, but it sure helped make some of the wild foods they gathered taste better. And their dad used the maple sugar and some herbs to make a sort of chocolate that wasn't that bad. It didn't really taste like chocolate but it didn't taste that bad either. It was sweet, at least.

It wouldn't be much longer

and it would be time to start

tapping the trees for sap again.

This time they would try to

gather twice as much so the

sugar would last all year.

After the maple trees came

the oak trees they gathered

acorns from in the fall. The

acorns had to be soaked in the

stream for a week before you

could grind them into flour or

they tasted terrible. But you

could pick up a bunch of them

and it wasn't that hard to do.

Their dad had tried to

make the acorn flour into bread but it wouldn't rise, even after he figured out how to get wild yeast, but he did figure out how to make a sort of tortilla with it that wasn't bad.

After walking another hundred yards through the woods, Sid suddenly stopped. He turned to Russel and made the hand signal for Danger, and pointed to a spot about 100 feet in front of him.

Russel followed with his eyes where Sid was pointing and

saw the danger his brother had spotted. The zombie looked like it had been an average sized man. It wore a dark colored long sleeved shirt and trousers.

Normally it would be difficult to see at night, but the white new snow and full moon made it easy to spot. The zombie was facing the other direction and hadn't spotted them yet. It rocked back and forth slowly, the way all zombies did when nothing was drawing their attention. Russel thought of zombies as "its" because they weren't people anymore and if he thought of them as "he" or "she", it made it harder to kill them.

The zombie seemed to be in decent shape. Russel guessed that it hadn't been a zombie very long, since its clothes weren't torn up or really dirty. Zombies were barely conscious and tended to bump into things or trip as they walked. It didn't take too long before their clothes were a mess.

Russel considered their

options for a moment. They could take a wide path around the zombie and avoid it. But they were going to be making noise digging later and there was no guarantee the zombie wouldn't hear them digging, or just happen to randomly walk that direction.

Plus the zombie's clothes looked to be in decent shape.

"Maybe there was still something useful in the pockets." Russel thought hopefully. Even pocket change could be pounded into useful shapes and sometimes they were carrying knives or even lighters.

Russel hesitated a moment longer, even though he had made up his mind to kill it. His pistol was loaded and ready, but he didn't want to take a shot and risk the noise bringing more zombies their way if he didn't have to.

Russel silently walked forward until he was standing about 20 feet in front and to the right of Sid, got the hatchet out of his belt, and gave Sid the hand signs for Short Light.

Sid turned on his flashlight and shown it for a second toward the zombie, which immediately began lurching toward him.

The zombie was focused on Sid and didn't even notice Russel swinging the hatchet at the back of its head as the zombie passed him. It was important to make the first hit count.

Zombies weren't any faster

or stronger than a regular person, in fact they were usually slower, but you still didn't want to get in a fight with one. The zombie dropped to the ground with a thud and lay still. Russel waited a full minute to make sure it wasn't dangerous any more, and then went through the pockets.

The only thing the zombie had in its pockets were a wallet with credit cards and car keys. Russel shook his head. "What in the world was a wallet good for?

How did this person survive for 3 years?" he wondered.

Russel pulled off the zombie's shoes, and tossed them to Sid to try them on. They were too big, but they were good quality leather shoes that still had quite a bit of wear left in them, so Russel cut strips of cloth from the zombie's pant legs for Sid to wrap around his feet before he put the shoes back on.

Sid stood up. "It's better. They don't hurt to walk in." Sid barely whispered. Russel nodded. It was the first time Sid had ever mentioned his feet had been hurting.

"He is one tough kid", Russel thought. "He should be tucked in a nice warm bed somewhere instead of walking through the woods at night to get food, but Sid never complains".

Russel wiped the hatchet blade off on the grass and hooked it back on his belt and motioned for Sid to take point again. Neither of them said a word as Sid resumed walking forward, drifting silently from tree to tree.

They walked for 10 more minutes when Sid froze. He made a sign for Russel to come forward and Russel silently crept up to where he could see what Sid saw.

Between the trees they could see an old man just sitting on the ground looking exhausted. He wore a dingy red and white suit, a big red hat, big black belt and black boots. The man had an unkempt white beard, but other than a general state of dirt and grime, he looked for all the world like pictures Russel had seen of Santa Claus when he was younger, before the zombies came and their lives had changed overnight.

Russel and Sid waited for a full half hour. The old man didn't move, and no one else seemed to be in the area.

Russel motioned to Sid to

cover him, and Sid got into position. Sid kept the pellet rifle pointed at the old man, but kept his head up so he could see the entire clearing. Sid knew there wasn't anything coming from behind him, but if they found the old man, someone or something might find him also.

It was always a risk to talk to someone, but the old man seemed unarmed and harmless. Maybe he had something worth bartering for, or had heard some news from other places. With

Sid covering him, Russel had some backup in case the unexpected happened.

Russel touched the small pistol he kept in the back of his belt. He was left handed, but sometimes the first sign of trouble was a bullet or knife in your arm. It was best to keep your weapons where you could reach them with either hand.

He raised his hands in the air in a non-threatening way and stepped out to where the old man could see him.

Chapter 3

Russel took a breath and tried to appear calm and confident. "Hello. I'm not going to hurt you. Got anything to trade?" Russel asked.

Russel waited while the old man seemed to consider the question. Russel glanced around the small clearing. The old man appeared to have no supplies of any kind, other than what he might have in his pockets.

He had no obvious weapons, and while his big red coat was certainly large enough to conceal nearly anything, with it buckled closed with that big black belt, it would be difficult to use a weapon quickly, if he even had one.

Russel shifted his balance from side to side as he waited. Most people would respond pretty quickly to any stranger, if only to avoid seeming weak and indecisive. Russel tensed up. This stranger was certainly behaving oddly, and Russel didn't want to be caught off guard in case the old man was more dangerous than he looked.

After almost a minute, Russel was about to ask again when the old man finally spoke softly.

"Trade? That's funny. I don't think I've had anyone offer me anything before. Maybe milk and cookies. Back when there was milk. And cookies. Don't tell me it's been so long you don't recognize me?"

Russel paused for a moment. He wasn't sure how to respond. Finally he said, "I know who you are trying to look like. It's been a while since I thought he was real though."

The old man sighed. "That's the problem young man.

No children left anymore. Oh, there are young kids out there, a few of them, but no CHILDREN. No one tells young children stories about me coming on Christmas anymore, everybody is working so hard just to stay alive that no one has time for the Christmas tradition anymore, so no children believe in me. And without the belief of children…I am just an old man. A very, very old man."

Russel laughed. "Old man, you have got to come up with a

better story than that. You've got the suit all right, but Santa Claus lives at the North Pole with a bunch of elves and a toy factory. If you were Santa, you wouldn't be here in the cold if you didn't have toys to deliver. You'd be in your nice warm house with all the elves."

The old man looked down at his lap and sighed. "Magic. All of it was magic. And it all went away as my magic faded." He said sadly.

"I don't have ANYTHING

without magic. No reindeer, no factories, nothing. When the last of it was fading I thought maybe if I came down here first and I don't know...I don't know what I was thinking. I packed up some supplies and came down south looking for some way to, I don't know. I guess I thought I would find an answer somehow, some way to fix everything. That was weeks ago. Now I'm out of food. I used to be able to be anywhere instantly and carry toys for every child, it's almost funny that I would just run out.

Now I've got nothing. No food, not even matches. A little magic is all it would take. But it's all gone now." The old man put his head in his hands and sighed.

Russel thought for a few minutes. The old man was clearly crazy, but probably harmless. Maybe he used to be a department store Santa or something and just lost his mind when the zombies came. He certainly wouldn't be the first person that couldn't handle the strain.

On the other hand, sharing food meant less for he and Sid. No one knew what the weather would be like in advance anymore. They could get snowed in and not be able to hunt for weeks.

Russel looked at Sid and Sid shrugged. Russel made up his mind.

"Old man, you are in luck. You are sitting in a patch of Sunchoke. There's enough here to get you through the winter. If you don't mind sharing, that is."

The old man looked up at Russel in disbelief. "You would share your food with a total stranger?"

Russel shrugged. If the old man was crazy, it wouldn't do any good to confront him about it. "You brought me and my brother toys for years. I figure I can get you through the winter. In the spring you can keep moving south, maybe find what you are looking for."

The old man blinked. "You believe me? You believe IN

me?"

Russel thought for a few seconds. It explained how he was still alive out in the woods alone with no supplies. No one would last long alone these days. Not in a red and white suit you could see for miles.

"If you aren't Santa" he said slowly, "You'll do till Santa comes along."

Russel motioned for Sid to come out. Russel and the old man took turns digging Sunchoke roots from the ground with the shovel while Sid kept a watchful eye for danger until they had a big pile.

Then Russel gathered pine resin from nearby trees and dead branches from trees that had died but hadn't fallen yet. He made a pile of tinder and sticks before chopping down larger branches and dragging over three larger logs.

Sid kept lookout while Russel used one of the few remaining matches from the emergency bag to start a fire and

then the three of them sat
around the fire, sat on one of
the logs and roasted the roots
over the coals from the other
two logs.

Sid and Russel
automatically sat back to back
on the log so they could see in all
directions, while the old man sat
back with his back against the
closest tree. The smoke drifted
up into the clear night sky, and
the sparks flew when the fire
snapped and crackled.

The sweet, nutty flavor of

the roasted roots tasted
wonderful to the hungry boys
and the heat from the coals was
just warm enough to be relaxing.
It was a beautiful crisp clear
night, and for a while it almost
felt like a cookout from the old
days.

While they sat around the
fire Russel and Sid told the old
man about how the scientists
thought the zombies were
caused by some unexpected
interaction between a new flu
virus and an older disease,

maybe rabies, but nobody really knew.

The doctors tried to save people, but they were among the first to die from the Zombies. It all happened so fast, there wasn't time to do anything but try to hide. Russel and Sid's family were among the first to get away from the cities so they didn't have to deal with the weeks of famine and violence, when millions were dying every day, but even for them it wasn't easy.

Everyone they knew died, one way or another. They didn't think to bring everything they needed. They had to hide from the waves of people trying to find safety, and then hide from the waves of zombies as eventually everyone got sick or infected.

"We were lucky. Our parents planned ahead and had food stored just in case." Russel explained. "Eventually we ran out, but it kept us safe during the Crazy Year."

"Where are your parents?"
The old Man asked looking
concerned.

"They left about a month
ago." Sid said quietly, then
quickly looked at Russel as he
realized his mistake. You never
gave anyone a sign you were
alone, no matter how friendly
they seemed.

"They will be back soon,
probably tonight." Russel said
quickly. "They left to get some
seeds so we could grow wheat
that we could plant this spring

and harvest every year. So we'd never be hungry again." Russel explained.

"And watermelons and sweet corn and radishes." Sid smiled a rare smile, then frowned again. "They thought the trip was too dangerous for us so we had to stay behind." Sid finished quietly with a sigh. "I miss them. It's lonely."

"I suppose it is." The old man said gently. His eyes made contact with Russel's and neither of them said what they were thinking, that the trip was very dangerous and their parents might not be coming back.

"We heard there were some kids our age about 100 miles south, but it's too dangerous to travel there just to meet them." Sid sighed.

"Very wise." The old man said as he nodded slowly with his head slightly tipped to the side.

Chapter 4

"How about you?" Sid asked. "Why are you alone? And why aren't you at the North Pole?"

Russel was surprised. Sid was talking more tonight than he had in the past week. Something about the old man was calming and reassuring. Maybe he really was Santa Claus.

"Well, during the Crazy Year, I did stay at my home at the North Pole. My magic showed me what was happening but… soon I just couldn't watch anymore."

The old man spoke slowly at first staring into the fire, then sighed before looking up at the boys and continuing on sadly. "I watched the Naughty and Nice book get thinner and thinner as everyone died. I watched everything around me fade as the children that believed in me died and the babies that survived weren't taught about me."

"At first I was still able to help, the few that still believed generated enough magic for that. I could at least bring food and supplies to the few that still believed. I tried so hard to help..." Tears rolled down the old man's cheeks.

"I wasn't what they needed. The children...they needed help. All I could do...all I did was watch and hide. I told myself that no one could ever see me, that it was a rule. That I could only visit once a year, on Christmas Eve, it was a rule. The truth is I stayed where it was safe. I hid while the children died."

The old man sobbed.

"There was nothing I could do. And when their names faded from the Naughty and Nice book when zombies killed them or they got sick I just watched. Until finally the book was empty, all the pages were blank. The children were all

gone." More tears rolled down

the old man's face. "And then

the book itself disappeared and I

guess I gave up hope."

"You did what you could."

Russel said gently. "You

aren't...."

Russel paused. "You're

nice...you're...Santa Claus."

The old man sighed and

wiped his face seemingly

without thinking about it, and he

continued on as Sid and Russel

sat and listened in silence, the

fire burning down to embers.

"I didn't have anything to do. Who am I without children to bring presents for? What was the point? I just sat up there, doing nothing."

"After that, bit by bit, everything else just slowly vanished. Each day there were fewer and fewer Elves to keep me company, then the workshop was gone and finally my house disappeared. I still had the reindeer and sleigh so I headed south. I tried landing in a couple of places, but there weren't any children, and there wasn't anything I could do.

I felt the magic fading and I took a chance on one more trip and got here. Now the reindeer and sleigh are gone and the only thing left are these clothes I have on. I guess the clothes are going to stay with me."

There didn't seem to be anything else left to say. They ate quietly as they finished dinner, then Russel got up and used his hatchet to chop down some pine branches and made a small shelter, while Sid went back to standing watch. Russel stripped the top and the branches from a small tree and made a seven foot spear before hardening the tip of the spear in the fire.

"Your clothes look warm, but in the daytime someone can see you from miles away. The zombies are attracted to bright colors and well…" Russel shrugged pointing at Santa's coat.

Santa listened intently as Russel gave him advice.

"Stay under the branches as much as you can during the day, sleep on the branches at night, they will keep you up off the ground. There is a creek for water a hundred yards to the east." He said, pointing across the clearing.   "We'll be back tomorrow night. Try to stay out of sight until we get back. Use this spear, it will be good enough to handle any zombies. Don't try to throw it, just hold it with

both hands and use it like a
sword, jab at them with it until
they stop moving. For tomorrow
just stay out of sight during the
day, keep the fire going and
don't panic and you'll be fine."

Santa listened and nodded
at everything Russel said, but
Russel wasn't sure the old man
had what it took to survive. He
seemed like a nice old man, and
there weren't any nice old
people around anymore.

Russel went back to digging
roots and as soon as they had

dug enough roots for the next day, Russel and Sid got ready to leave. Russel picked up all his equipment and slung the bag of roots over his shoulder before turning to Sid and giving the "let's go" hand sign.

Sid shocked Russel by running up and giving the old man a hug before picking up the pellet rifle and heading out.

Russel picked up the spear again and handed it to Santa. "Merry Christmas, Santa. Keep one hand on it all the time.

Sleep with it beside you. Stay alert and you'll be ok." Russel wasn't sure that Santa would really be ok, but it seemed like the right thing to say.

Santa seemed to stand up straighter. "A Christmas present! Thank you, Russel!"

Russel thought the old man's clothes suddenly seemed cleaner, somehow. His belly seemed to fill out the big old coat more. Russel shook his head and decided his imagination was getting the best of him.

Santa watched as Russel followed his brother out of the clearing. Santa realized he was standing up straight, hands on his hips, just like in the old days.

"Goodbye Santa." Russel turned, just before stepping out of sight. "I hope you find what you are looking for someday."

The old man smiled. "You know, I think I will." He smiled as Russel and Sid walked away through the woods. "I really think I will."

Chapter 5

Russel and Sid walked back
to their camp in silence, drifting
from tree to tree. The trip back
took longer as they made sure to
take a different route back. It

wasn't a good idea to take the same path each time.

If someone saw their tracks, they might be waiting for them to return the way they came. The moon was just starting to go behind the tree line and soon it would be time to get a few hours of sleep.

Showing that old man where the Sunchokes were meant they would be scrambling all winter, hunting more and taking more risks to find food. The winter season would be a lot harder than they were planning.

There was no way of knowing when their parents would return, and there wasn't any way for their parents to bring much food in addition to the seeds, if they did find any seeds.

There weren't any other options, they would have to risk scavenging in the empty houses now. Maybe they would find something that was missed before, or something they could trade for food.

The acorns they had harvested were almost all eaten, along with the cattail roots and cattail pollen they had collected earlier in the year, and it would be at least a couple of months before the dandelions and other edible weeds came up in the spring. Russel grimaced.

His dad had said the inner bark on most pine trees was edible. That sure didn't sound like it would taste very good, but even eating pine bark was better than an empty belly.

Russel thought hard.
Maybe he could make some
more traps and catch some small
animals. Maybe he could take
the electrical wire from the
abandoned houses and use it
somehow. Or maybe try to
catch some fish. The water was
freezing cold now, but maybe he
could dig up more cattail roots.

Russel sighed to himself.
Sure, and maybe a deer would
wander up to him and wait for
him to shoot it.

The boys worried together

in silence, they both knew what the other was thinking.

When they reached their cabin, the boys walked the outside perimeter to make sure there weren't any zombies tangled up in the fence and then the quietly stepped inside the small cabin.

As they stepped inside, Russel lit a lamp with a burning ember from the wood stove and added another small log.

Satisfied the fire would keep going, Russel turned

around and froze. Sid stood

there silently, neither of them

believing what they were seeing.

By the glowing light of the

lamp they could see there were

cases of chili and soup,

preserved cheeses and meats,

bags of rice and beans, enough

food for them to live on for

months, all stacked up neatly in

the far corner of the small cabin,

along with two new sleeping

bags and two new pairs of boots

and gloves. And perched on top

of it all were books for Russel

and Sid's favorite toys.

Sid turned to Russel, "I knew it! I knew it! I knew that was Santa!"

Russel watched in amazement as Sid ran over to the pile laughing with joy. Sid laughed and danced around the pile, spinning in circles as he held up each toy before collapsing on the floor giggling. After a minute, he got up and grabbed a bar of chocolate. Real chocolate! He grinned at Russel from ear to ear as he happily unwrapped the bar and quickly began eating it.

Russel looked at the pile and just shook his head. Food. Boots. Sleeping bags. Matches. Thick cotton socks. Clean socks without holes! Russel rocked back and felt the soles of his shoes through the holes of the socks he was wearing and imagined pulling on new socks, and the feeling of socks that would keep his feet warm...

And books! Some were his favorites, others he hadn't read

before. All of them looked brand new. Russel turned the books over in his hands, feeling the smooth covers and running his fingers over the edges of the books.

Taped to one of the books was a small piece of paper with something written on it. Russel turned the note towards the light from the lamp. The handwriting very ornate, but Russel could easily read it. He got Sid's attention and read the note aloud.

"Russel and Sid,

Your parents are fine, they will be back in a few days.

I'm headed south, to find those children you boys talked about and as many more as I can. It's time I stopped hiding and started helping again. Children need my help. They need something to believe in. And I need to help them.

Your parents aren't going to believe you, and that's ok. Children will. Tell all the Children. Santa will come if they believe.

Thank you so much,

Santa"

Russel's eyes teared up with joy and relief and he wiped them off on his sleeve of his jacket.

At the sound of bells ringing in the distance the boys ran outside. The boys looked up just in time to see a flying sleigh pulled by reindeer disappear in the distance.

Just as the sleigh

disappeared from sight, they

heard a deep voice shout

"Goodbye to you both! And

Merry Christmas!"

What did Russel and Sid eat to survive?

There weren't any grocery stores or even gas stations anymore. So where did Russel and Sid find food? In the spring, summer, and fall the answer was, nearly everywhere. About one out of three plants are edible, and about one out of three of those taste good enough to eat. Be careful though. Many plants will make you sick if you eat them, some may even kill you. So always know what you are eating before you eat it.

A big challenge with living on wild plants is that they usually don't have a lot of calories, which is where you get your energy to run around and keep warm in the winter. If you look at cows in a pasture, they are almost always eating or chewing.

That's because they have to eat or chew constantly to get enough calories from the grass they eat. Humans can't use the nutrients in grass as well as cows can, so we would have to eat even more of it. It would take so much grass that we can't survive on eating grass, although it can help keep you from feeling hungry.

The parts of the plants that have the most calories and protein are the pollen (which is hard to harvest from anything but a cattail), the seeds and the roots. The green leaves of many plants are edible and in many cases are downright tasty, but you would have to eat 8 to 10 pounds of green leaves a day to get enough protein. Talk about a belly full of leaves! So eat the leaves if you must, but when zombies come remember to focus on harvesting the seeds and roots.

Here are a few of the plants that are easy to recognize and are common in many places. They may not taste familiar, but if zombies come, they may be all you have to eat! Just remember, until zombies come, the ditches beside the roads will often be sprayed with chemicals, and even after the zombies come the ditches beside big highways may have a lot of lead in the soil. So always harvest plants that are at least 100 feet from a road and watch out for areas that people might be spraying chemicals.

These are just a few of the plants that Russel and Sid ate to survive. It's a good idea to learn about the plants that are common in your area. It won't help to learn about plants that you can't find!

Make a list of the plants in your area and research how to cook and eat them. Make absolutely sure you know what you are eating before you eat them. If you can, find someone in your area to show you which plants are which and how to tell them apart.

Acorns:

Acorns are easy to recognize and depending on the type of oak tree can be a great source of starch, fats and protein.

Start by dunking the acorns in water, and throw away any that float. These are hollow because bugs have eaten part of the insides!

Take the rest out of the water and let them dry. Put a container of clean water nearby and start splitting them open with rocks or a hammer, whatever you have. Be careful not to smash your fingers! The water doesn't have to be ready to drink because you are going to boil it anyway, but it should be fresh and clear.

Pop the acorn meat in the water quick, so it isn't exposed to the air any longer than it has to be. When the container is 1/3 full of acorns (or you are out of acorns), boil them until the water gets dark, then pour out the water, add more fresh water and boil them again. Keep doing it until the water doesn't get dark when you boil it. Now all the bitter tannins are gone and the acorns are ready to dry out and grind into flour or eat roasted or in soup.

There are lots of types of oak trees though, so keep track of which tree you get your acorns from. You may find some acorns in your area taste better and are easier to prepare. If you don't like how they taste, try another tree!

Amaranth or pigweed:

This is a very common plant, much to the dismay of many farmers. You can find Amaranth flour in many grocery stores (They don't call it Pigweed in grocery stores, people might not buy it) but you can find it growing in the ditches by fields, in pastures, maybe even in your own backyard!

The seeds are high in protein, will give you lots of energy and are easy to harvest. Just place a bag over the top of the mature plant and shake the stalk. The seeds and some dry stuff will fall right into the bag. The seeds will stay good to eat for a long time as long as you keep them dry. You can eat them raw, cook them or grind

them into flour and cook with it!
Pigweed pancakes, yum!

In the spring, you can eat
the young plants raw or cook
them and they have lots of
vitamins! In the summer the
bottoms of the plants will be
pretty tough, so just eat the
tops. But don't eat them all, you
want to leave some plants to
make seeds later!

Cattails:

Cattails grow pretty much anywhere there is water, are a great source of calories and are an easy plant to harvest.  Some say you can get more food from an acre of cattails than an acre of potatoes and the cattails plant themselves!

Keep an eye on the brown parts that look like a hot dog on a stick. In the early summer when they turn yellow, they are producing pollen and that pollen is an amazing source of nutrition that tastes good too! Just put a bag over the top of the stalk and shake. You can gather a day's worth of food in an hour or less if you have a good patch and work fast. You can eat the pollen any way you want. Mix it with other flours to add protein and nutrition to your bread (And make it taste great too!) or add it to any soup or broth for a colorful and nutritious boost to your diet.

In the fall and winter you can harvest the roots. Just remember the water gets pretty cold in the winter, so you may want to harvest as much as you can in the fall while the water is warmer!

Reach down into the muck and loosen the roots with your hands, so you get as much as you can. Wash them off as best you can and then peel them. Smash them into pulp and swish the pulp around for a few minutes until the starch is all in the water. Strain out the fiber and let the water settle for a few hours and the flour will settle to the bottom. Pour off the water, and dry the remaining paste into flour.

Remember, any plant that you harvest from under water has to be cooked before it's eaten or you can get sick, so always make a bread or soup from the cattail flour, don't just eat it!

If you don't have a container and can't make flour from the roots, you can roast them over a fire. Just remember you can't digest the fiber, so chew it good to get the starch, then spit out the fiber from every bite. You can't digest the

fiber and it can give you a
bellyache!

Turn the page for a sneak peek
at the next installment in the
Russel and Sid Adventure Series

The Crazy Year

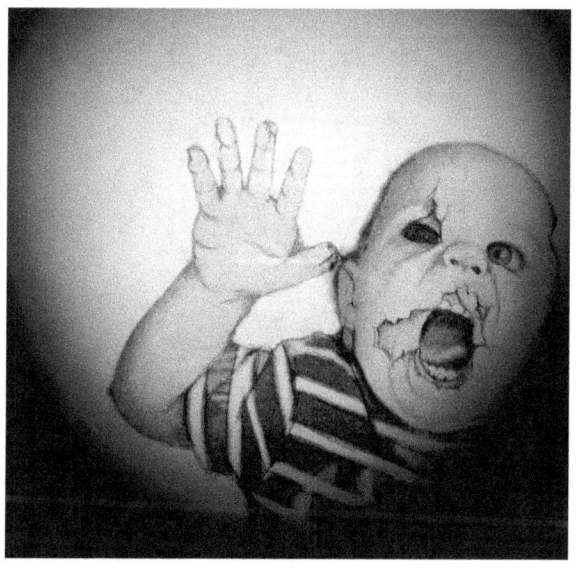

Coming soon from Washmet
Publishing!

Russel and Sid stood side by side, looking out the picture window at their neighbor who was getting out of their car. Since the schools were closed and they weren't supposed to leave the house, they spent most of their time looking out the windows watching the neighbors.

"Dad, I think Mr. Wilson has got Stupid!" Russel called out, as their neighbor dropped a bag of groceries tried to close the car door while trying to hold four large bags.

"Why do you say that?" His dad asked, joining them at the big bay window.

"He just dropped a bag of groceries!" Russel replied.

Their dad looked for a moment while their neighbor struggled to pick up the fallen bag while holding three other bags before saying, "Well, that's not really that bad. Let me know if he can't figure out how to open his front door or starts licking his cat or something."

The boys laughed as their dad turned and walked a few steps back toward the kitchen.

"And call them sick or something. Stupid just sounds bad." Their Dad said as he turned back towards them.

"That's what the people on TV are calling it. They are saying everyone is getting Stupid!" Sid said excitedly.

"I know. But I think the people on TV are getting…might be sick. This has to be a disease, everyone can't just be getting dumb all at once. Something has to be making their brains not work right or something." Sid and Russel's dad walked back into the kitchen.

Sid and Russel continued watching their neighbor drop groceries while trying to pick up the items on the ground.

"You know, he wasn't that smart before. I bet he is just

having a bad day." Sid said matter-of-factly as their neighbor dropped more groceries as he chased a can of coffee that was rolling across his driveway.

Russel watched intently as their neighbor kneeled down to pick up the can of coffee between two bags of groceries, while he dropped another bag.

"You may be right. Remember when he forgot what day it was and put the garbage out on Tuesday?" Russel asked, as Mr. Wilson triumphantly picked up the can of coffee and dropped the rest of the groceries.

The boys watched as their neighbor carefully set down the coffee, unlocked the front door and left the coffee on the step.

"This seems worse." Sid said thoughtfully.

"Let's tell dad. Race ya!" Russel said as he took off running.

"No fair, you got a head start!" Sid complained as they ran through the house.

The boys burst into their dad's office, with Russel barely in front.

"Dad, dad, dad!" The boys yelled together.

"He has definitely got stupid!" Russel said conclusively. "He forgot all the groceries!"

"Even the coffee!" Sid chimed in.

"Guys, quiet! There's a news update." Their dad said, making a shushing gesture with his hands as he watched the news on his laptop screen. The boys waited quietly while their dad watched the screen intently.

They didn't understand everything they were saying on the news, but it sounded bad. Russel heard "Sleeping Sickness" and "Rabies" and what sounded like "Algae virus" but that couldn't be right, could it? Did algae get viruses?

Russel decided he would look it up that evening. Russel wanted to be a biologist when he grew up and his parents often found him researching different plants and animals late at night when he was supposed to be sleeping.

The boy's father turned back to the boys with a tired look on his face. "They don't even know for sure yet if it's a disease or something else. If they haven't identified the virus yet, or if it's a virus, they haven't even started looking for a cure."

Russel and Sid looked at each other. Their dad looked worried, and that was never a good sign.

About the Author

     Patrick Kilhoffer graduated from Illinois State University with a degree in Economics. He and his wife started a national marketing company which they later sold and he is now semi-retired in Danvers Illinois with his wife, Tori, and two sons, Riley and Simon, and a parrot that wanders around the house looking for him when it gets bored.

     Patrick still helps businesses with their marketing but spends most of his time researching, writing, riding his bicycle, distributing food to those in need and preparing for the inevitable zombie apocalypse.